Don't Go In The Cellar

by

Jeremy Strong

Illustrated by Scoular Anderson

You do not need to read this page -
just get on with the book!

Published in 2004 in Great Britain by
Barrington Stoke Ltd, Sandeman House, Trunk's Close,
55 High Street, Edinburgh, EH1 1SR

This edition based on *Don't Go In The Cellar*, published by
Barrington Stoke in 2003

ISBN 1-84299-211-2

Printed in Great Britain by Bell & Bain Ltd

Meet The Author – Jeremy Strong

What is your favourite animal?
A cat
What is your favourite boy's name?
Magnus Pinchbottom
What is your favourite girl's name?
Wobbly Wendy
What is your favourite food?
Chicken kiev (I love garlic)
What is your favourite music?
Soft
What is your favourite hobby?
Sleeping

Meet The Illustrator – Scoular Anderson

What is your favourite animal?
Humorous dogs
What is your favourite boy's name?
Orlando
What is your favourite girl's name?
Esmerelda
What is your favourite food?
Garlicky, tomatoey pasta
What is your favourite music?
Big orchestras
What is your favourite hobby?
Long walks

Find out more about Jeremy Strong and his books ... visit his website:
www.jeremystrong.co.uk

Contents

Chapter 1
The Writing on the Wall

"Why must we have Laura to stay?" said Zack.

"Because her mum is my best friend and I want to help her out. She has to go away for a few days," Zack's mum told him.

"But I don't like Laura."

"You don't have to like her. She's sort of family."

Zack went up to his room and sat on his bed. Laura was coming to stay. There was no getting out of it. Zack did not like Laura. This was why:

1. She was a girl.

2. She was clever.

3. She had pushed him into the paddling pool. (OK, he was only four at the time.

He had got wet. Very wet. And Laura had had a big laugh.)

4. Laura had pushed Zack into the paddling pool. So Zack had pushed her into the flower bed. Then Zack had had a big laugh, but not for long. Mum's best flowers had been smashed.

Zack's mum had been very cross with him. She hadn't been cross with Laura. This was not fair. Laura had pushed him first. It was the first time that Zack saw how unfair life could be.

Now they were both 12 and Zack still didn't like Laura. He sat on his bed and felt cross.

There was so much stress in Zack's life at the moment. His family had just moved into a new house. It was a long way from their old home. There was a new street and

new faces next door. Then there was a new school, new teachers, a new town, a new job for Dad and so on and so on. Now, when they had only been in the new house for three days, Laura was coming to stay.

Zack gave a big sigh. He lay on his side and stared at the wall. It was a fine day and the sun was shining into his bedroom. In the bright light, Zack saw some words on the wall that he hadn't seen before.

The writing was low down on the wall. The letters were very small and done with felt tip. This is what they said:

Do not go in the cellar

Just that.

Do not go in the cellar

Zack sat up in bed. *I've seen this message before*, he thought. They had found an old wardrobe in his bedroom when they came. Zack had looked inside. There was nothing in it, but on the back of one of the doors some words had been cut into the wood.

Do not go in the cellar

The odd thing was, the new house didn't have a cellar. So what was going on?

Chapter 2
Laura

"Laura's here!" Zack's mum called up to him. He knew she'd come. He had heard the taxi drive away then the doorbell ring. His mum had been talking to someone.

"Come down and say hello," Zack's mum called up to him. She smiled at Laura. "Zack's a bit shy," she said.

Up in his room, Zack heard what his mum had said and went very red. Why did parents always get these things wrong? Why did they do this to him? Zack shut his eyes and counted to ten. Then he went down.

"Hi," said Laura. "I like your new house." She smiled and her face lit up. Zack said hello in a low voice.

"My, how you've grown," said Zack's dad to Laura as he took her bag.

Why do people always say that? Why do they bother? thought Zack. *Of course she's grown! That's what children do as they get older! We haven't seen her for eight years!*

But he didn't say a thing. He walked slowly behind Dad as he took Laura round the new house. While she looked at the rooms, Zack looked at her. *In fact, she has grown*, he thought. *I didn't think she'd be like this.*

She was almost as tall as he was. Her hair was still black, but now it was so long she had to keep pushing it back to keep it out of the way. She smiled all the time.

Zack's dad showed Laura her room. "That's Zack's room along there," he said, "and you'll be in here."

Zack had an idea. "Show her the cellar, Dad," he said.

Dad shook his head. "He keeps asking me that, Laura. And I keep on telling him there isn't one. I think he's having some kind of joke with me, but I don't think it's very funny."

Laura smiled and Zack felt angry. Mr Dawson went down to the kitchen and they were left alone.

"Why do you want to see the cellar?" asked Laura.

"Because there isn't one," Zack told her.

"Do you always talk in riddles?" asked Laura.

For a moment Zack was silent. Should he show Laura the message on the wall?

In the end he felt he had to tell her.

"Come and see something," he said, and they went to his room.

First he showed her the wardrobe. "This was the only thing that was left in the room when we got here," he told Laura. She read the words cut into the door.

"How do you know it means this house?" asked Laura. "It could have been written inside the wardrobe before it got here."

"I'd worked that one out for myself," said Zack. "But just lie down on the bed," he said.

Laura giggled. "Do you fancy me, then?"

Zack went bright red. He almost yelled at her, "No, I don't fancy you! But I want you to read something. You can only read it if you lie on the bed close to the wall."

Laura smiled and lay down on the bed. Zack moved a lamp so that it shone on the words on the wall.

"Do not go in the cellar," read Laura. She sat up and looked at Zack. "Well," she began, "it must be under the house somewhere. How exciting! It's just like Harry Potter. Come on!"

Zack walked slowly after her. Somehow he felt his life was being taken over.

Chapter 3

The Cellar

Zack and Laura looked for the cellar for hours. Mrs Dawson was amazed how well they seemed to be getting on.

"I think Zack's quite keen on Laura," she told Mr Dawson.

"How can you tell? He snaps at her all the time."

"That's what I mean," Mum said. "Of course, Zack doesn't *know* he's keen on her."

Mr Dawson looked at her and shook his head. "Women are so odd," he said. He watched Zack and Laura walk past the window. "So if Zack's keen on her, is she keen on him?"

"Oh, yes! Laura's liked Zack since she was four! That's why she pushed him into the paddling pool!" Mrs Dawson told him.

Mr Dawson shook his head again. "I shall never understand women," he said.

Luckily, Laura and Zack didn't know that Zack's parents were talking about them. They had far too much to do looking for the cellar. They had been all over the house but so far they had found nothing.

They went into the garden and tried to find a door to the cellar outside the house.

"It could be anywhere," said Zack.

"Not anywhere," said Laura. "It's got to be near the house. In fact, I expect it's right up against the house wall. What about in the greenhouse?"

"It's full of junk," said Zack.

"I know. Come on." Laura pushed her way into the greenhouse. It was very small and full of old planks and piles of pots.

"This is more of a dump than a greenhouse," said Zack.

Laura looked hard at the corner where the greenhouse joined on to one wall of the house. It was piled high with old junk.

"Help me get rid of this lot. It might be behind here," said Zack. The big planks were hard to lift. Everything had to be

moved around the greenhouse so that they could get into the corner.

"Well, well, well," said Zack. For there was an old door. In fact, it was more like half a door. It started low down and only came up to their chests. But it *was* a door. Someone had painted a message on it in large red letters.

Do not go in the cellar

"I think we'd better go in," grinned Laura.

"Do you always do what you're told not to do?" asked Zack.

"Of course," she said. She turned the handle and pushed hard at the door. She almost fell inside as it flew open, and Zack had to grab her to stop her falling down the

dark steps on the other side. He pulled her back and she fell against him.

"You're so strong," Laura said, and gave him a sweet smile.

"Oh, shut up," said Zack, and led the way down.

The smell was old and stale but it was not a bad smell, just different. They were standing in a small room. A very large, dusty machine filled all the space. There were cobwebs everywhere. The machine had great big wheels with lots of cogs to make them go round. Huge metal rods and giant chains linked the wheels. There were levers for lifting things and pistons to move up and down.

At the far end of the room was a big metal chest. What could be inside? On one side was a large lever. On top of the chest was a dirty glass window, the size and shape of a letterbox. Zack rubbed the window clean. He looked inside but it was blank.

"I don't know what that window is for," he said.

"How about this?" asked Laura, with her hand on the lever. "What does this do?"

"We mustn't touch it," said Zack.

So Laura pulled the lever. She *had* said that she always did what she was told not to do. The machine began to creak and roar. The wheels turned. The chains clanked. Pistons shot to and fro. The floor began to shake. There was a noisy CLUNK and a word came up in the dirty window. Zack looked at it. It said:

HORROR

"What does that mean?" asked Laura
with a grin.

A moment later she found out.

A skeleton jumped on her back.

Chapter 4

Horror

"Aaargh! Aaargh! Get it off me!" yelled Laura.

Zack grabbed a broom. He hit out at the clacking bones until they fell in a heap around Laura's feet. She stared down at the pile of bones in horror. Then, all at once, they got themselves back together and went off, clicking as they went. Laura's face was very pale.

"What's going on?" she said in a
whisper. She looked around in panic. But
the cellar was silent and still. Two eyes
shone in the dark. Then four eyes, six eyes,
a hundred eyes. Laura clung to Zack. Zack
clung to Laura. "We're being watched," she
said. "Who are they? What do they want?"

"Walk towards the steps, very slowly,"
Zack said softly.

Voices began to whisper in the dark.
There seemed to be lots of them. They

chattered and licked their lips. "Zack? Laura? Come over here. We want to eat you. Oh yummy yum! Oh yes! An arm for me and a leg for you! Yum yum yum!"

Laura and Zack got to the bottom of the steps.

"Run for it!" yelled Zack, and he pushed Laura in front of him. They raced up the steps and almost fell into the sunshine. Zack looked around. It was all right. Everything was back to normal. No skeletons. No monsters. They were safe. Zack hoped Laura could not hear his heart thumping.

"You're a mess," he told her, as he brushed the cobwebs from her hair.

She gazed back at him with big, wide eyes.

"You saved my life," she said.

Zack didn't know what to say.

"Zack? Laura? It's lunchtime. Come on!"
Mrs Dawson called from the house.

She sounded so normal. It was what they
both needed to hear. They just wanted to
forget what had happened.

"Come on, lunch is on the table," called Mrs Dawson again from the kitchen.

"Don't say a word," Zack said to Laura as they went in.

"Your mum would think it was just a silly story anyway," she replied.

Zack sat at the table in a daze. He'd saved her life? He wasn't so sure. He didn't feel as if he'd saved her life. He felt muddled – very muddled.

"So, how are you two getting on after all these years?" asked Mr Dawson. Zack gave a shrug. Mr Dawson winked at his wife. Zack saw the wink, and sank into an angry silence.

"I've made a pie," said Mrs Dawson. She opened the oven door, reached in and gave a yell. She yelled and she yelled and she yelled.

It was not a pie that came out of the oven. It was a huge, hairy spider, as big as an octopus. Its giant legs clicked and clacked as they looked for food. It had very large jaws and eight huge, round eyes. One eye looked at Zack. One eye looked at Laura. One eye looked at Mrs Dawson and the other five stared at Mr Dawson.

Mr Dawson jumped up and slammed the oven door, shutting the spider in. He turned up the heat. A weird howl came from inside the oven. There was a strong smell of sizzling hair.

Mrs Dawson was shaking all over. She pointed to the oven. She couldn't say a thing. Her hair stood on end. Laura gripped Zack's hand under the table.

Zack gulped. "So, no pie then," he said, and tried to smile. "What's for pudding?"

Laura gazed round the room. First a skeleton, then a giant spider. What *was* going to happen next? "The walls!" she gasped. "Look at the walls!"

The kitchen walls seemed to be coming alive. They were moving and shaking, as if something was about to burst through. Little holes appeared, like little dots, getting bigger and bigger. And out of the holes came ...

Giant slugs – slugs as big as a man's arm.

Mr Dawson ran to Mrs Dawson and threw his arms around her. "What do we do?" they yelled.

"Quick!" cried Laura. She pulled at Zack and dragged him outside. "We must get back in the cellar and turn off the machine!"

Chapter 5
The Story Machine

They almost fell down the steps.

"Quick!" panted Laura. "Help me push the lever back to where it was!"

They grabbed the rusty lever and pushed as hard as they could, but there was no way they could get it to go back.

"It can't be done!" cried Laura.

"We can't just give up," Zack told her. "Mum and Dad are being attacked by giant slugs. Come on – let's see if it will move the other way."

They pushed at the lever once more. Slowly it began to move. *CLUNK!*

A new message flashed up into the little window. Laura and Zack looked at it.

FAIRY TALE

Laura frowned and looked at Zack. "Fairy tale?" she asked. Zack took a quick look around the cellar. No skeletons. Phew! Things seemed to have gone back to normal, if only for a moment or two.

"I think I know what this is all about," Zack began slowly. "I think this is some kind of story machine. It makes different kinds of stories. The first kind was horror, and now it's ..."

"... going to make a fairy tale," nodded Laura. "That will be why there's a dragon behind you."

Zack turned round fast, only to see something very small scuttle away behind the old table. Zack smiled and relaxed. It was a dragon all right, but it was very small. Poor thing! It must be scared of them. Zack made clucking noises and held out his hand to the little dragon. He picked it up.

Laura watched and held her breath. *How could Zack pick the dragon up? What if it tried to bite him? What if it could breathe fire?* All at once her heart almost stopped. *WHAT IF THE BABY DRAGON'S MOTHER WAS JUST AROUND THE CORNER?*

Just then there was a loud crash. Some bricks fell out of the wall and a knight in shining armour came crashing into the room. He was waving a huge sword. The broad, blue blade shone as he swung it round and round.

"All right, where's the dragon?" he boomed. "I know there's a dragon in here. I am Sir Knight-in-Shining-Armour and this is my sword, Dragon-Cutter. It always glows blue like this when a dragon is near. I must slay it at once."

"But it's just a baby," said Zack, holding the little dragon close. The knight strode towards him. Zack felt the wind as the sword cut the air above his head.

"Babies grow up!" roared Sir Knight. "I am the dragon slayer! Hand it over at once!" He stepped forward and held his sword high above his head. Zack shrank

back before him. He knew that both he and the baby dragon were going to die.

Laura tried hard to think. What could she do? Then her face lit up. Yes! It might work! She ran to the bottom of the steps and began to wail and moan and pull at her hair.

The knight turned to her at once. "What? A poor princess in distress? I must save her at once." He strode across to Laura and went down on one knee before her. "Fair princess," he began, "what's the matter? Are you about to be eaten by wolves? Is a wicked wizard about to turn you into a frog? How can I help you?"

"Oh, woe is me," said Laura, as if she was a poor princess. She put her hand to her head and gave a groan. "There are huge slugs in the kitchen and they are about to eat my friend's mum and dad! Only you can save them!"

Zack was amazed. *Hmmm*, he thought, *she's cunning. She's saving me and my parents all in one go. That's a clever trick!*

"Do not fear!" cried Sir Knight-in-Shining-Armour. "I shall slay those slimy slugs and we shall all live happily ever after!"

"You are my hero!" said Laura, with a sigh. Zack didn't like that much.

Sir Knight-in-Shining-Armour charged up the stairs, and Zack and Laura ran after him. Outside they saw that something odd was going on.

There was a crowd of people round Zack's house, and they seemed to be eating it.

Chapter 6

The Pie Arrives at Last

"Hmmm, this is good gingerbread," said one man, as he munched away at one of the walls of the house.

What he said was true. The walls *were* made of gingerbread. The roof was cake icing. The door was made of chocolate. Of course people were eating the house.

The giant slugs had gone. Zack's parents were marching up and down, trying to pull

the people away from the house. They were very cross.

"Don't do that," they were saying. "This is our house! Stop eating our front door!"

All at once there was a loud crash and the garage fell to bits. One wall had been eaten away by the crowd.

"They're eating us out of house and home," cried Mrs Dawson. "I don't understand it. First we had a giant spider, then slugs, and now our house is being eaten as we stand here. And why is there a knight in shining armour clanking about the place? Oh, it's all too much."

Zack and Laura looked at each other and nodded. "Back to the cellar," said Zack. "How long is this going to go on for, do you think?"

Laura gave a shrug. "I haven't a clue. Come on, we'd better hurry, or there'll be nothing left of your house."

Back in the cellar, they pushed at the lever once more. *CLUNK!*

"What does it say?" Zack asked. He felt nervous.

"SLAPSTICK," Laura read out. "What do you think that means? Urffff!"

A custard pie came out of nowhere and landed slap bang in her face. She wiped the

custard away from her eyes and gave Zack
an angry look.

"Did you do that, Zack? I'll get you!"
Laura rushed at him, slipped on a banana
skin and fell flat on her face.

Zack was having a good laugh. "It's like
the circus, Laura!" he yelled. "It's very
funny."

This made Laura even crosser.

She got up and set off after Zack again.
He turned to run. There was an awful noise
as the back of his trousers ripped on a
sharp nail.

"Oh, no!"

It was Laura's turn to laugh. "I can see
your pants!" she cried, jumping up and
down. "I can see your pants!"

Now it was Zack's turn to chase Laura.
She ran up the steps and out into the
garden, where a pie war had broken out.
Pies of every sort and size were flying all
over the place. An apple pie landed splat on
Zack's chest. A cream tart hit him bang on
his ear. A jet of tomato ketchup got Mr
Dawson on the head.

Mrs Dawson had one foot stuck in a
bucket. Laura was wet all over. Zack had
aimed a hose at her. He didn't even know
he had a hose in his hand. This was so
weird!

And then Zack saw what was happening
to the house. It was no longer made of
gingerbread. It was a real house again, but

– and it was a very big BUT – one whole side of the house was falling over.

One whole wall was falling towards them. It was going to crush them. "Look out!" yelled Zack. "Look out!"

They all stopped and stared as the wall came rushing towards them, rushing, rushing, until ...

CRASH!

Zack shut his eyes. The wall hit the
ground with a thud. Could it be true? He
was still there. He was still alive. He looked
around. By some amazing good luck
everyone had been standing where a
window frame had landed. They stood
there, in the window frames, with the wall
lying all around them. They looked at each
other in amazement.

"Wow," said Laura, with a little smile.
"That was lucky!"

"You've got custard in your hair," Zack told her.

"Pants!" Laura snapped back, and Zack, without thinking, put both hands on his bottom.

Chapter 7

Buckets of Blood

"Can someone please tell me what's going on?" asked Mr Dawson. "It's like some odd dream."

"More like a nightmare," said Mrs Dawson.

"It's the cellar," Zack began.

"There isn't a cellar!" cried his father. "Stop going on about it."

"There *is* a cellar," said Laura. "We've been inside it. There's a machine down there making all these things happen, and we can't get it to stop. Everything has to be slapstick at the moment, and that will go on until we change it."

"What comes after slapstick?" asked Mrs Dawson.

"That's just the problem," Zack told her. "We don't know until we push the lever."

By this time all four of them were down in the cellar. They were trying to get to the machine. They had to fight their way past the piles of banana skins, flying pies and jets of water. On top of that their trousers kept falling down.

They all pushed on the lever. *CLUNK!*

MURDER MYSTERY

"Oh dear," said Mrs Dawson. "I don't like the sound of that."

There was a scream and a dead body landed on the table beside Mrs Dawson. There was a thud as it hit the table, and blood rained down all over her.

The dead man had an axe stuck in his head, an arrow in his heart and a dagger in his chest.

"Aha!" cried a stern voice from the far corner of the cellar. "You did that, Mrs Dawson, didn't you? I am the Great Detective and I arrest you for the murder of Lord Plummy."

"But I didn't do it!" Mrs Dawson told him.

"Then why is there so much blood on your hands? It's red too, just like Lord Plummy's blood!"

"All blood is red," said Zack.

"And I arrest you too, Zack, for helping your mother to murder Lord Plummy," cried the Great Detective.

"But, sir, they can't have done it," Laura told him. "They were both with me."

The Great Detective took a step back. "They were with you? Aha! Can you prove it?"

"Of course I can, because I was with ... *him*!" Laura pointed at Mr Dawson. The

Great Detective frowned. "And you, sir," he said. "Where were you?"

"I was with you," Mr Dawson told him.

"Aha! ... I mean, what? Really? With me?" the Great Detective said, amazed. "But, but, but that means *I DID IT!* I am the murderer!"

The body on the table sat up. There was blood everywhere. Lord Plummy gave a sigh.

"You are all useless," Lord Plummy told them. "None of you did it. The butler stabbed me. The gardener shot me with his bow and arrow, and then I stuck an axe in my head."

Lord Plummy got off the table and splashed across the cellar to the machine. "I'm fed up with all this murder. Look what it's done to my suit. Blood everywhere!

Well, it's jolly well going to stop." He pulled the lever. *CLUNK!*

Everyone else crowded round the little window and stared at the next word.

Chapter 8
Don't Look!

ROMANCE

That was what it said. Romance.

Zack had a quick peek round the room. His mum and dad had gone. He was alone with Laura. The cellar was full of sunshine. A bluebird sang in one corner. Some butterflies flew past. The sweet smell of roses filled the air. He could hear a splashing waterfall.

Laura smiled at Zack. "You're so brave," she said softly. "And good-looking."

Zack gulped. He wanted to say: *Keep away from me!* He wanted to say: *What's going on?* He wanted to yell: *HELP!* But he simply couldn't do it. His mouth opened and he heard himself say, "I think you're the most beautiful girl I've ever seen."

This was an odd thing for Zack to say, because by this time Laura looked a mess. She still had bits of pie and tart all over her, as well as a lot of Lord Plummy's blood. Her face and hair were filthy. But Zack thought Laura looked beautiful, and he told her so.

"You haven't always liked me, have you?" asked Laura, taking a step closer to Zack.

He shook his head. "You pushed me in the paddling pool," he said.

"And you pushed me into the flower bed," she replied.

"You pushed me first," Zack said.

"I only pushed you because I liked you," said Laura. "I've always liked you," she added, and came a step closer.

Zack couldn't move. He wasn't sure now if he wanted to run away or wait and see what would happen next.

Laura came even closer. He could hear her breathing. She held out a hand to him. She lifted her face to his. She pressed up to him and he stepped back. *CLUNK!*

He had pushed the lever. It was as if Zack had been woken from a deep dream. He backed away from Laura fast. Could it be true? They had been going to kiss! Him and Laura!

Laura was gazing at the glass window. "It's empty," she said. "It doesn't say anything. It's over."

"Thank goodness for that," said Zack. "Come on. We have work to do."

He took Laura by the hand and pulled her up the stairs and out of the cellar. Together they pulled the cellar door shut. Zack nailed a big plank of wood across it. He found an old paintbrush and a tin of paint. He set to work with the brush and added two more words to the message on the cellar door, one at the start and one at the end.

DEFINITELY

Do not go in the cellar

EVER

"That'll do it," he said.

Zack and Laura went out into the garden and fell onto the grass. They were worn out by it all. Zack felt the warm sunshine on his face. He turned to Laura. He could see her face, but her eyes were closed. Had she gone to sleep?

Oh well, he thought, *she's OK for a girl. In fact she's ...*

Laura's eyes were open and she was gazing at him.

"We've had a lucky escape," he said. "Who knows what might have happened?"

"Who knows what *will* happen?" said Laura, and she put a hand on his arm. "Who knows?"

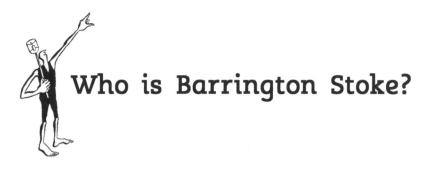

Who is Barrington Stoke?

Barrington Stoke went from place to place with his lamp in his hand. Everywhere he went, he told stories to children. Some were happy, some were sad, some were funny and some were scary.

The children always wanted more. When it got dark, they had to go home to bed. They went to look for Barrington Stoke the next day, but he had gone.

The children never forgot the stories. They told them to each other and to their children and their grandchildren. You see, good stories are magic and they can live for ever.

If you loved this story, why don't you read ...

Problems with a Python

by Jeremy Strong

Have you ever looked after a friend's pet? Adam agrees to look after a friend's pet python, but things get wildly out of hand!

4u2read.ok!

You can order this book directly from our website
www.barringtonstoke.co.uk

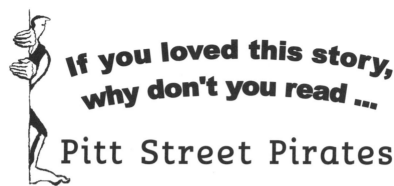

If you loved this story, why don't you read ...

Pitt Street Pirates

by Terry Deary

Have you ever dreamed of finding a long-lost treasure? Meet the Pitt Street Pirates – a group of friends with just one thing in mind – to sail the lakes in their local park in search of gold. But how will they put their plans into action? And can they stop The Rich Kids from getting there first?

4u2read.ok!

You can order this book directly from our website
www.barringtonstoke.co.uk

If you loved this story, why don't you read ...

The Two Jacks

by Tony Bradman

Are you always getting told off at school? Or are you the teacher's pet? Jack Baker is the perfect pupil until a new teacher mistakes him for bad boy Jack Barker!

4u2read.ok!

You can order this book directly from our website
www.barringtonstoke.co.uk

If you loved this story, why don't you read ...

The Hat Trick

by Terry Deary

Is there something you'll remember for as long as you'll live? When Seaburn football team meet their rivals, Jud has to step in as goalie. Can Jud save the day?

4u2read.ok!

You can order this book directly from our website
www.barringtonstoke.co.uk

If you loved this story, why don't you read ...

Wartman

by Michael Morpurgo

Have you ever had a wart? Dilly has one called George who causes him a lot of grief. Until that is, he meets old Mr Ben.

4u2read.ok!

You can order this book directly from our website
www.barringtonstoke.co.uk

If you loved this story, why don't you read ...

Problems with a Python

by Jeremy Strong

Have you ever looked after a friend's pet? Adam agrees to look after a friend's pet python, but things get wildly out of hand!

4u2read.ok!

You can order this book directly from our website
www.barringtonstoke.co.uk